First U.S. edition 1993
Published in Great Britain in 1993 by Walker Books Ltd., London.

Library of Congress Cataloging-in-Publication Data

Alborough, Jez.
Clothesline / Jez Alborough.—
1st U.S. ed.

Summary: The animals have hung their clothes of all shapes
and sizes out on the line to dry and the reader can guess which item
belongs to which animal by lifting the flaps on each page.
ISBN 1-56402-243-9
1. Toy and movable books—Specimens. [1. Animals—Fiction.
2. Clothing and dress—Fiction. 3. Toy and movable books.] I. Title.
PZ7.A323Cl   1993
[E]—dc20   92-54962

10 9 8 7 6 5 4 3 2 1

Printed in Hong Kong

The pictures in this book were done in markers.

Candlewick Press
2067 Massachusetts Avenue
Cambridge, Massachusetts 02140

CLOTHESLINE

Jez Alborough

CANDLEWICK PRESS
CAMBRIDGE, MASSACHUSETTS

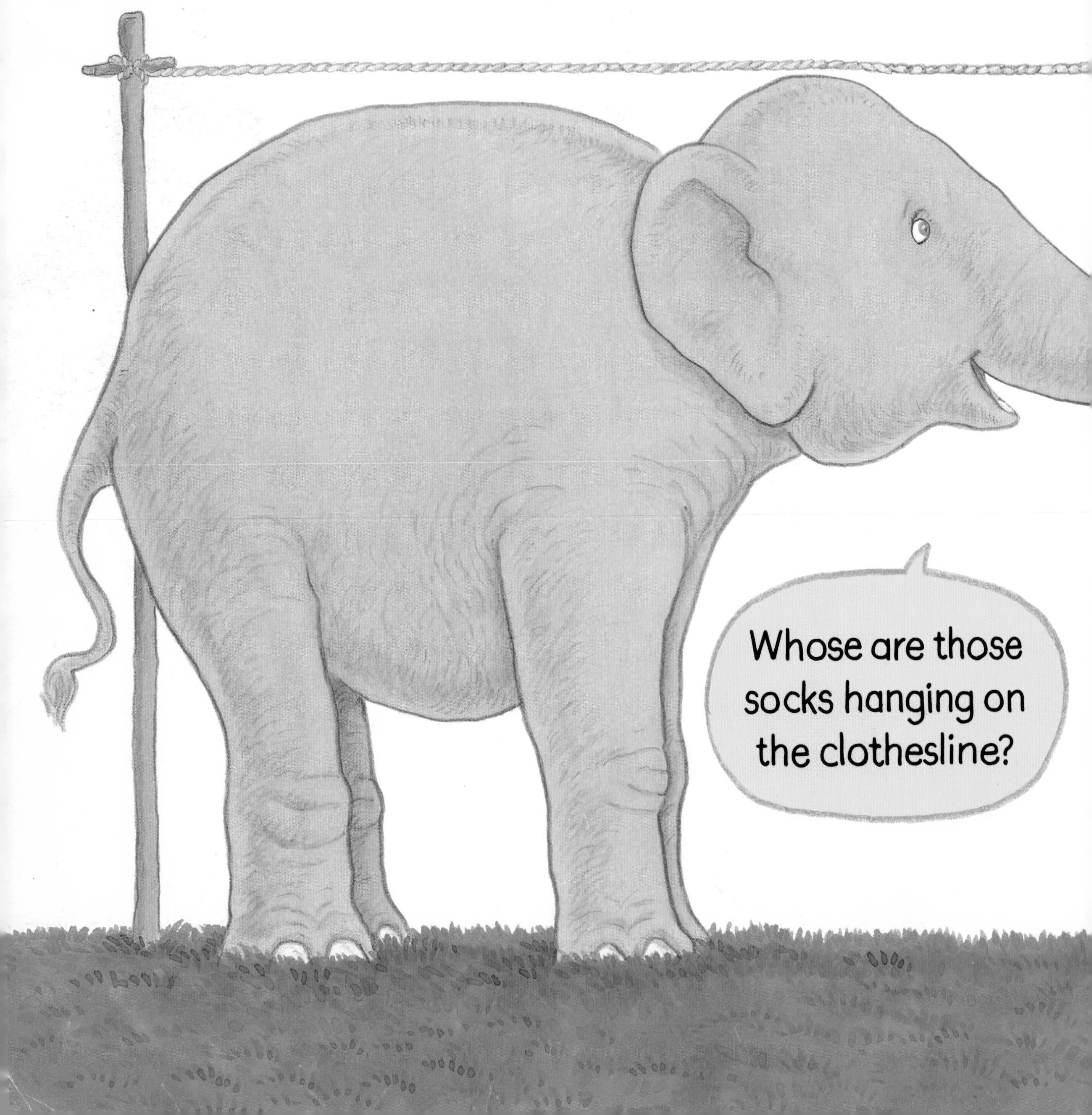
Whose are those socks hanging on the clothesline?

asked the elephant.

asked the elephant
and the flamingo.

grunted the
orangutan.

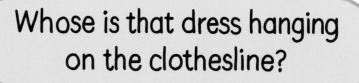

Whose is that dress hanging
on the clothesline?

asked the elephant,
the flamingo,
and the orangutan.

asked the elephant,
the flamingo,
the orangutan,
and the mouse.

Whose are those underpants hanging on the clothesline?

asked the flamingo,
the orangutan,
the mouse,
and the giraffe.

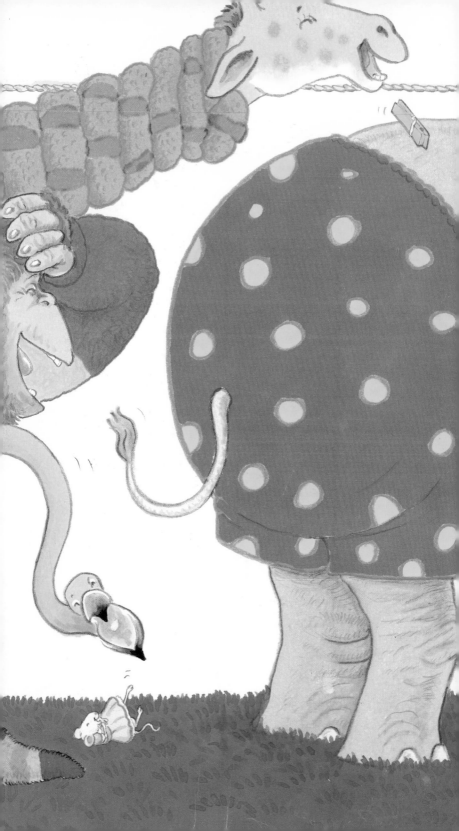

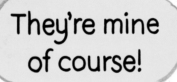

said the elephant.

What are we going to do now that we're all wearing our dry clothes?

asked the flamingo,
the orangutan,
the mouse,
and the giraffe.

I have an idea

said the elephant.